MARVEL
SUPER ADVENTURES
READ-AND-PLAY STORYBOOK

MARVEL

New York
Los Angeles

SUSTAINABLE FORESTRY INITIATIVE | Certified Sourcing | www.sfiprogram.org | SFI-00993 | This Label Applies to Text Stock Only

TABLE OF CONTENTS

"Spider-Man vs. the Green Goblin" based on the Marvel comic book series *Spider-Man*.
Adapted by Steve Behling. Illustrated by The Storybook Art Group.

"Wolverine vs. Silver Samurai" based on the Marvel comic book series *X-Men*.
Adapted by Alison Lowenstein. Illustrated by Val Semeiks and Hi-Fi Design.

"Iron Man vs. Crimson Dynamo" based on the Marvel comic book series *Iron Man*.
Adapted by Steve Behling. Illustrated by Craig Rousseau and Hi-Fi Design.

"Hulk vs. the Abomination" based on the comic book series *Hulk*.
Adapted by Clarissa Wong. Illustrated by Val Semeiks and Hi-Fi Design.

ISBN 978-1-4847-0435-6   V381-8386-5-14003   Printed in the United States of America
First Edition   1 3 5 7 9 10 8 6 4 2
© 2014 MARVEL

It was just another day at Midtown High School. Peter Parker was reading about his alter ego, **the amazing Spider-Man**, in the *Daily Bugle* newspaper.

"What are you looking at, bookworm?" said Flash Thompson, a bully at school.

Peter ignored him. Then Peter's friend Harry Osborn ran over. "Hey, guys!" he said. "**The Enforcers** have broken into the Empire State Building!"

As Spider-Man, Peter had faced the Enforcers before. They were **cunning criminals**! Peter dashed into a nearby alley.

Seconds later, Spider-Man was swinging high above the streets of New York City! **He was ready for anything.** But he had a strange feeling that someone was watching him.

Spider-Man soon arrived at the Empire State Building.
The Enforcers were expecting him! Montana tried to
snare Spider-Man with his lasso. But Spidey dodged the rope.

Next, Ox tried to throw a garbage can at the hero, but Spidey spun a web and stopped him!

Then Dangerous Dan threw a strange grenade at the web-slinger, but it did not seem to harm him.

Spidey used his webs to tie up the Enforcers.

As he swung away, he yelled to the police, "They're all yours, officers, courtesy of your friendly neighborhood Spider-Man!"

Peter changed back into his regular clothes. He felt like he was being watched. His spider-sense usually warned him of any danger, but this time it didn't. The Green Goblin had given Dangerous Dan the grenade. **It was filled with a gas that weakened Peter's spider-sense!**

The Green Goblin followed Peter back to his house.
The Super Villain knew Spider-Man's secret identity!
"Do not go inside, Spider-Man," the Green Goblin hissed, "or
I will just have to drag you out!"

The Green Goblin attacked! Without his spider-sense to warn him of danger, Peter could not dodge the Goblin's blasts. He soon grew tired.

"You're not so fast now, web-head!" the Goblin hissed as he captured Peter!

When Peter Parker woke up,
he found himself trapped inside
the Green Goblin's secret lair.

"Take a look, Parker—this is the last face you will ever see!" the Goblin said as he took off his mask.

Peter could not believe it. The Green Goblin was **Norman Osborn**—his friend Harry's father!

Peter knew he had to distract the Goblin to break free. Peter hoped getting him to talk would work.

"So how did you become a villain, Gobby? Did you win a green costume in a contest?" he said. **That made Norman angry.**

"I will tell you how I became the Green Goblin!"
Norman said. "I was experimenting with a strange
chemical formula. It suddenly turned green and exploded!"
The explosion gave Norman great strength. He
decided to use his new powers to become the greatest
costumed criminal of all.

"And now it is time to defeat you forever!" said the Goblin. He freed Peter so he could prove that the Green Goblin could beat Spider-Man. Peter put on his Spider-Man mask. **It was web-slinging time!**

The Goblin threw a pumpkin bomb at Spider-Man. "Did you forget the powers I possess?" he said.

Spidey spun a web at the Green Goblin's face. "How can I forget?" he said. "You keep talking about them!"

Blinded by the web, the Green Goblin
stumbled backward. He knocked over many
vials of chemicals, causing a **huge explosion**!

As the smoke from the explosion cleared, Spider-Man rushed over to
the Green Goblin. Norman looked at Spidey, but he didn't recognize him!

He didn't remember that Spider-Man was Peter Parker! Instead, he only asked about his son, Harry.

Norman Osborn was no longer the Green Goblin. **Spidey had saved his friend's father.** And his secret identity was safe, too. All in a day's work for your friendly neighborhood Spider-Man!

Wolverine was visiting his martial arts instructor, **Sensei Edo**. Edo was a peaceful man. He wanted to use his skills to teach people who could help others.

"Professor X and the X-Men think I'm a master fighter, but I know there is more to learn," Wolverine confessed to Sensei Edo as they walked through a path lined with cherry blossoms on **Philosopher's Walk**.

Suddenly a figure appeared before them, surprising Wolverine!

The silver figure grabbed Sensei Edo, who fought back, but was overpowered.

It was **Silver Samurai**! And he had taken Sensei Edo.

Wolverine had to stop him. Sensei Edo might be a martial arts expert, but he was no match for a powerful mutant like Silver Samurai.

Wolverine ran after Silver Samurai. He had to save Sensei Edo! He could see them heading into the streets of Kyoto.

"You'll never get away, Samurai!" Wolverine shouted.
"Just watch me!" Silver Samurai screamed back as he raced through Nishiki Market.

Pow! Wolverine threw his foe into a barrel of pickles. Shoppers stopped to stare at the commotion.

Wolverine didn't know what Silver Samurai wanted with the old man, but he knew that it was up to him to stop the **evil mutant**!

Just then Silver Samurai leaped onto the **bullet train** platform. With Sensei Edo in tow, Silver Samurai quickly jumped atop the train. The train moved at **lightning fast speed**.

Wolverine raced toward them! He scaled the side of the train, using his claws to help him make his way to the top.

"Let him go," Wolverine demanded. "Samurai, Sensei Edo will not train any of your evil minions."

"Your wish is my command, Wolverine!" The train came to an abrupt stop and Silver Samurai **threw Sensei Edo off the train**.

Wolverine looked down at Sensei Edo,
who signaled to Wolverine that he was okay.

"I never wanted your teacher," Samurai told Wolverine. "I wanted you. You shouldn't have come to Japan, Wolverine. You aren't wanted here. **I was hired to destroy you.**"

Wolverine and Silver Samurai's battle
grew so intense that they **fell off the train,**
landing in the middle of the train station.

The two mutants could withstand powerful blows, but Wolverine was fierce and Samurai was losing his strength.

Silver Samurai used his ring to **teleport away from the fight**. Wolverine followed him before the portal could close!

Silver Samurai used his armor to deflect Wolverine's claws.
"I came here to learn," Wolverine said, trying to reason with
Silver Samurai and end the battle. "We don't have to fight."

"No!" cried out Silver Samurai. **"I will prove I am the best!"** He lashed out, and knocked Wolverine to the ground.

Suddenly Sensei Edo appeared behind Samurai. Edo said,
"I should have realized sooner. **I remember you, young man**.
You were also my student. It pains me to see you fight Wolverine."

"I'm not your enemy!" Wolverine pushed Samurai against a tree. Wolverine used his claws to knock Silver Samurai's sword away.

"It was my mission to capture you, Wolverine," said Silver
Samurai. "If I return without you... I do not know what will happen."
  "I came here to learn how to better protect my friends," said
Wolverine. "Maybe you could try doing the same thing?"

"Yes, I want to study with you," Silver Samurai replied. "Thank you for giving me another chance."

At the dojo, Wolverine and Silver Samurai sparred, but this time it was with Sensei Edo watching and teaching them new martial arts moves. Wolverine was pleased to see that **even the fiercest foe was able to become an ally**.

"You call that thing a *dinosaur*?" said Happy Hogan. Happy was talking to his boss, **Tony Stark**. Tony was a brilliant inventor who ran his own company.

"Not a dinosaur," said Tony. **"The Dyna-Soar.** A new spacecraft that will carry astronauts to the Stark Space Station and back. Today is the first test!"

The Dyna-Soar was almost ready for launch! The **mighty engines** began to roar, and Tony watched with excitement.

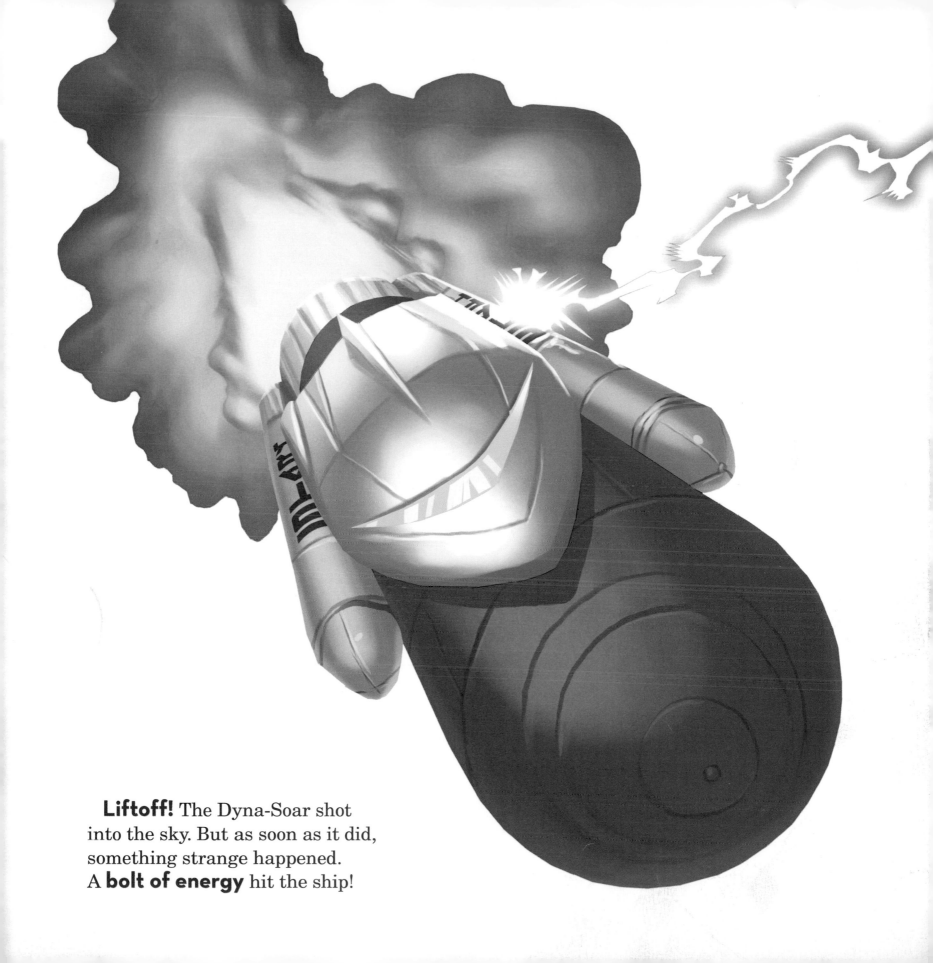

Liftoff! The Dyna-Soar shot into the sky. But as soon as it did, something strange happened. A **bolt of energy** hit the ship!

Tony knew that the astronauts inside were in **danger**.

He slipped away so he could change into his **Iron Man armor**.

With his **powerful jet boots**, Iron Man
quickly caught up to the spacecraft.

Soon, he started to get control of the ship. But it took all his strength, and his armor's power supply was getting **lower and lower**!

The Dyna-Soar shot down to Earth
like a meteor. Iron Man used nearly
all his energy to save the astronauts!
His armor had very little power left.

But before Iron Man could do anything else, he found himself under attack! "Face your doom," said the strange armored figure. **"Face the Crimson Dynamo!"**

The Crimson Dynamo's blast hurt Iron Man. The Armored Avenger fired his **repulsor rays** at his foe, but they did not do anything!

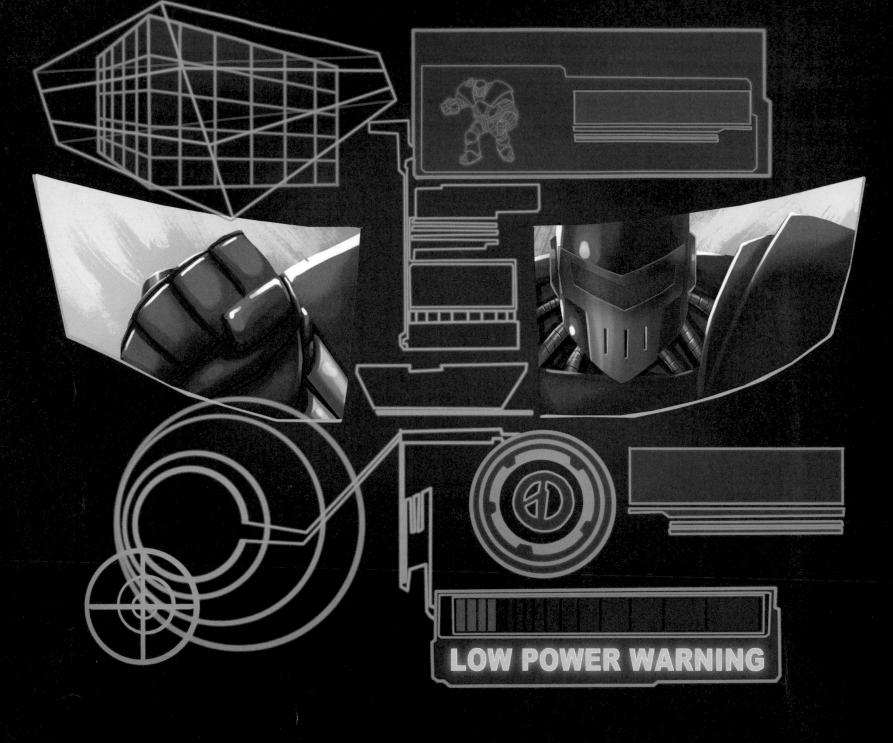

Iron Man watched the Crimson Dynamo come closer. Tony
was alarmed to see that his **armor was nearly out of power!**
How could he stop someone as strong as the Crimson Dynamo?

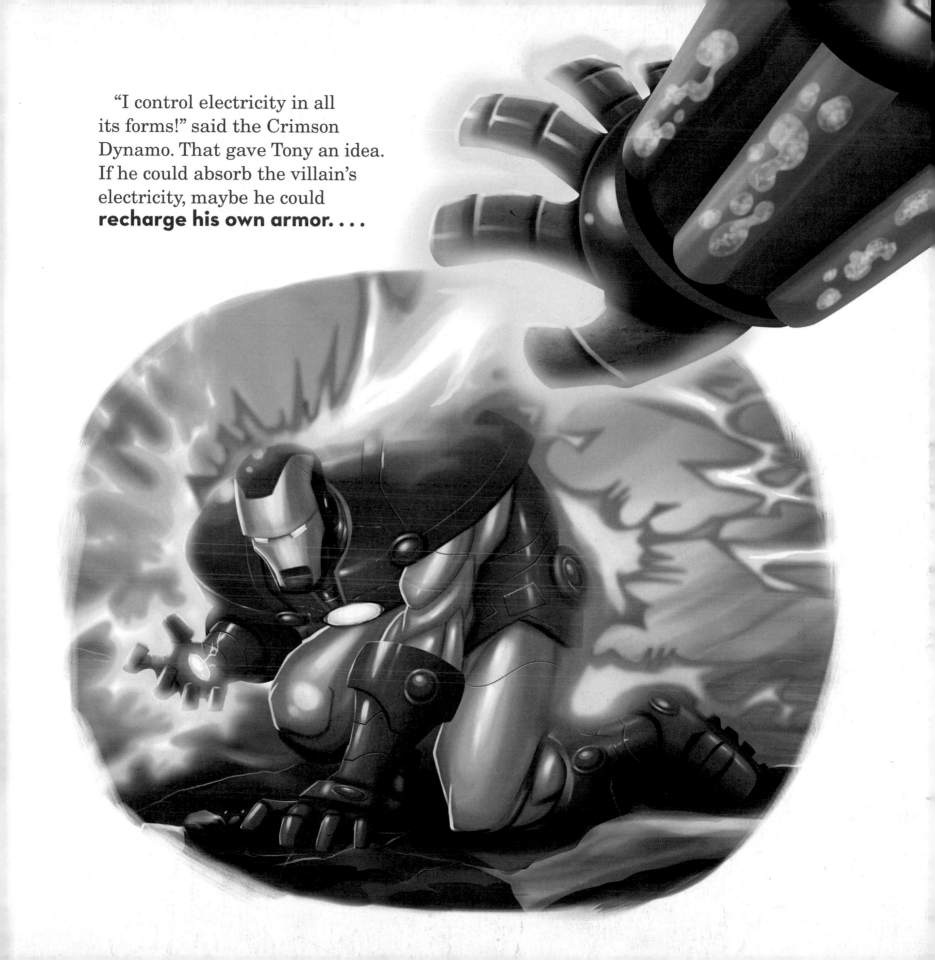

"I control electricity in all its forms!" said the Crimson Dynamo. That gave Tony an idea. If he could absorb the villain's electricity, maybe he could **recharge his own armor. . . .**

Tony made a change to his repulsor rays. Suddenly, the Crimson Dynamo **unleashed all his power**.

Unknown to the Crimson Dynamo, Tony was **absorbing energy**! With every blast, Iron Man was growing stronger.

Iron Man grew so strong that he had enough power to **stop the Crimson Dynamo** and send him soaring into the sky!

Against all odds, **Iron Man saved the day**! The
villian had been defeated and the astronauts were saved.

Bruce Banner was on the run from the Army. General "Thunderbolt" Ross was trying to **catch Hulk**. But maybe, if Bruce could stop changing into Hulk...there would be no need to run.

Hulk was created by Bruce experimenting with gamma rays. Bruce thought he could use altered gamma rays to make Hulk go away **forever**.

Bruce snuck into a science lab. Just as the gamma-ray machine was warming up, a soldier named Emil Blonsky noticed what was happening. He caught Bruce.

"Trying to escape?" the general asked with a smirk. He was very happy to finally have caught Bruce. "Boys, put him away before he can change into Hulk!" the general ordered.

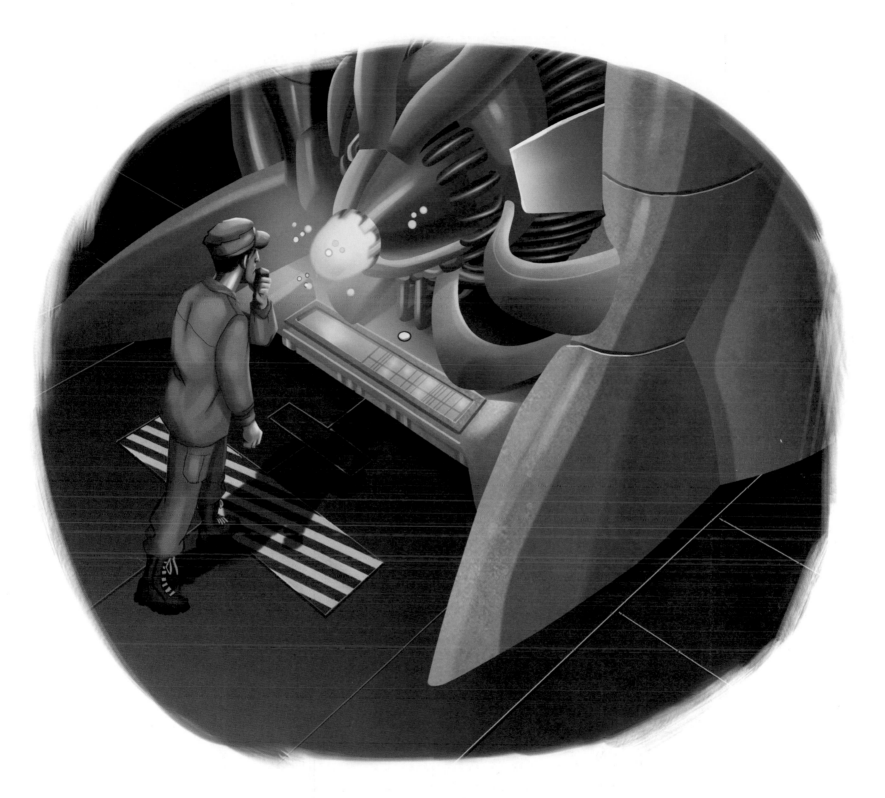

I wonder what that mad scientist was up to, Emil said to himself. Emil accidentally stepped on a button on the floor and **activated the machine**.

"What—what's happening to me?" Emil said.
His skin turned green and scaly, like Hulk's.

He was superstrong and filled with rage. He destroyed the machine,
because he did not want anyone else to be as powerful as he was.

"Ha! Now there is only me and that brainless Hulk!" Emil said with an evil laugh. "But soon... **only one will remain**."

Emil barged into the room where General Ross and his guards
were watching Bruce. At the sight of another green monster,
Bruce realized Emil must have been changed by the gamma rays.

"What is that...Abomination?" General Ross yelled.

"I am here to crush you all!" the new green giant growled.

The Abomination grabbed hold of Rick Jones, who was Bruce's friend. Rick was in danger! Suddenly, Bruce transformed into **the incredible Hulk**!

"Hulk SMASH!!!" Hulk cried out.
"My intelligence is greater than
yours"—the Abomination laughed—
"and so is my strength!"

"No one beats Hulk...no one!"
Hulk shouted.
"Fine, I'll use both hands!"
The Abomination tossed Rick
into the air!

Swiftly, Hulk caught Rick in midair.
"Hulk makes sure Rick is safe," Hulk said
as he put Rick down gently.
"Thank you!" Rick said.

The Abomination hit Hulk with
a mighty punch.
The Abomination was strong,
but **Hulk would not give up**!

"We have to do something, General!
Hulk saved my life," Rick said.
"Get the experimental Gamma
Cannon!" General Ross ordered.

"See how much stronger, smarter, and better I am than you?" the Abomination taunted Hulk. "No one can beat me!"

"Not so fast, Abomination!" the general shouted, pointing the device at the Abomination's chest. General Ross zapped the Abomination with gamma rays, weakening the evil beast.

As the Abomination staggered, the incredible Hulk head-butted the Abomination with all of his might. The battle over, **Hulk changed back to Bruce Banner.**

"General, what did you do to the Abomination?" Bruce asked.

"The Army built a new gamma-ray machine to use against you. But the Abomination was a greater threat than Hulk," the general replied.

"The machine we built was far from perfect. Looks like we wont be able to use it again. **I suggest you leave now,**" the general said sternly.

General Ross was uncomfortable letting Bruce go, but he knew the incredible Hulk had saved everyone.

"Don't make me tell you twice." The general looked over at Bruce.

Dr. Banner was happy that he had kept control and saved the day. Looks like Hulk can be a **force for good** after all, he thought.